My First SIGHT WORDS and SENTENCES

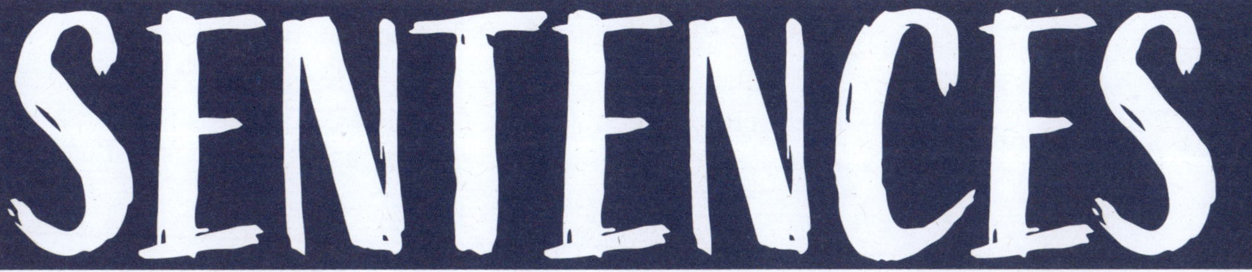

MOONSTONE

Published in Moonstone
by Rupa Publications India Pvt. Ltd 2025
7/16, Ansari Road, Daryaganj
New Delhi 110002

Sales centres:
Bengaluru Chennai
Hyderabad Jaipur Kathmandu
Kolkata Mumbai Prayagraj

P-ISBN: 978-93-6156-766-7
E-ISBN: 978-93-6156-143-6

First impression 2025

10 9 8 7 6 5 4 3 2 1

Printed in India

Table of Contents

Chapter 1:
Introduction to Sight Words

Definition

Sight words are the most commonly used words in the English language. These are words we often see in books, stories, and everyday reading. Because they appear so often, it's important to learn them by sight—meaning, you recognize them immediately without having to sound them out.

Examples of sight words:

a, and, the, is, it, you, said, come, here.

Why Can't We Sound Out Sight Words?

Sight words don't always follow the usual rules of spelling or phonics.

For example:

- The word "**said**" doesn't sound like how it's spelled.
- The word "**the**" cannot be sounded out easily.

Activity: Spot the Sight Words!

Look at the words below. Circle the ones that are sight words:

apple, **the**, **is**, **run**, **said**, **big**, **because**, **blue**, **cat**, **you**.

Fun Fact!

Did you know that sight words make up about **50% of the words we read?** That means knowing these words can help you read half of any book!

Why Are Sight Words Important?

Benefits of Learning Sight Words

1. **Reading Becomes Faster**
   - When you know sight words, you can read sentences quickly without stopping to think about each word.
2. **It Helps Understand Stories**
   - Sight words help connect ideas and make sentences complete.
     - Example: "**The cat is under the table.**" Without sight words, the sentence wouldn't make sense!
3. **Builds Confidence**
   - When children master sight words, they feel proud and excited about reading.

Quick Check: Can You Read These Sentences?

Underline the sight words in the sentences below:

1. I like to run and jump.
2. The sun is big and bright.
3. Can you see the bird?

How Many Sight Words Should I Know?

Here's a rough guide:

Age	Approx. Sight Words to Know
4-5 years	20-50
6-7 years	100+

Types of Sight Words

Common Categories of Sight Words

Helping Words

Words like **is**, **are**, **was**, **were**.

- Example: **She is happy**.

Pointing Words

Words like **this**, **that**, **these**, **those**, **here**, **there**.

- Example: **This is my book**.

Action Words

Words like **go**, **come**, **play**, **run**, **jump**, **eat**.

- Example: **I like to play**.

Connecting Words

Words like **and**, **but**, **because**

- Example: **I am happy because it is sunny**.

Practice Time: Match the Word to Its Type

Draw a line to connect the sight word with its category.

Sight Word	Category
is	Helping Words
this	Pointing Words
play	Action Words
and	Connecting Words

Practice Makes Perfect!

Activity 1: Fill in the Blank

Complete the sentences with the correct sight word:

1. I ________________________ happy. (is, am, are)
2. The dog is ___________ the table. (on, under, over)
3. Can you __________________ me? (see, jump, eat)

Activity 2: Circle the Sight Words

Circle the sight words in blue and the other words in red.

is, apple, the, run, you, dog, said, ball, here, book.

Activity 3: Read Aloud

Practice reading these sight word sentences:

1. The bird is in the tree.
2. I can jump and run.
3. Here is my red ball.

Words to Remember

Here are some of the sight words you learned today:

the, is, and, you, said, here, there.

Chapter 2: Recognizing Common Sight Words

What Are Common Sight Words?

Common sight words are the words that appear most frequently in books, sentences, and stories. Learning these words is the first step toward becoming a confident reader.

Some examples of common sight words:
a, **and**, **the**, **is**, **it**, **you**, **said**, **for**, **was**, **he**, **she**, **we**, **I**.

Why Are These Words So Important?

They Are Everywhere:
Sight words are used in almost every sentence.

They Make Sentences Complete:
Imagine reading without words like "**is**" or "**and**."

How to Spot Sight Words

Look for Short Words: Many sight words are 2-4 letters long.

- Examples: **is**, **the**, **and**, **you**.

Focus on Words That Repeat: Words like "**the**" appear many times in a book.

Check the Context: Sight words often connect other words.

- For example: "**The dog is happy**."

Activity: Highlight the Sight Words!

Below is a sentence. Highlight or underline the sight words:
I am here to see the dog and cat play.

Tips to Make Learning Easy

Practice Reading Aloud

Say the word out loud while pointing to it in a book.

- Example: "This is a dog."

Use Flashcards

Write one sight word on each card.

Show the card and say the word aloud.

Repeat Often

Repetition helps you remember. Try reading the same list of sight words every day.

Did You Know?

The brain remembers words better when you say them out loud and see them at the same time!

Activity: Fill in the Missing Sight Word

Choose the correct sight word to complete each sentence:

1. She ______________ a big ball. (**is**, **has**, **and**)
2. The cat is _________ the table. (**on**, **in**, **and**)
3. I ________________ going to play outside. (**am**, **is**, **are**)

Fun Activities for Learning Sight Words

Make Sentences

Combine sight words to form simple sentences.

- Example: "I am happy."

Sight Word Hunt

Search for sight words in books or on signs during a walk.

Activity: Match the Sight Words

Match the sight words with their pictures:

Sight Word	Picture
jump	
eat	
play	

Practice and Review

Read These Sight Words

Practice reading this list aloud:

the, **is**, **and**, **you**, **said**, **here**, **there**, **was**, **I**, **she**, **he**.

Write a Sentence

Use these sight words to create your own sentences:

- **I**, **am**, **happy**
- **The**, **dog**, **is**

____

____

____

____

____

____

Remember!

- Practice a little every day.
- Use fun methods like games and flashcards.
- Always read aloud to make learning easier!

Chapter 3: Basic Sight Words

What Are Sight Words?

Sight words are words that appear frequently in everyday reading. They are essential because they help us quickly understand what we're reading. Unlike most words, these are often difficult to sound out because they don't follow regular phonetic rules. Instead, we recognize them by sight.

For this set, we will focus on **9 basic sight words** that are commonly used:

a, an, the, is, it, in, on, at, and.

Why Are These Words Important?

1. **They Are Everywhere:**
   These words show up in almost every sentence we read. Mastering them helps us read faster and better!
2. **They Help Us Understand Sentences:**
   Words like "**the**," "**is**," "**at**" make sentences complete. Without them, the sentence would not make sense.
3. **They Are the Building Blocks of Sentences:**
   Understanding how to use these words allows us to create simple sentences, forming the foundation for more complex sentences later on.

Fun Fact:

Did you know that "**the**" is the most frequently used word in the English language? It's everywhere!

Sentences Using Sight Words

Activity: Fill in the Blank

Complete the sentences using the correct sight word:

1. She is ________________ the playground. (**at**, **on**)
2. I see __________________________ apple. (**an**, **a**)
3. The cat is ___________________ the box. (**in**, **on**)
4. The dog ____________________ running. (**is**, **are**)
5. I like to read _________________ books. (**and**, **a**)

Here Are Some Sentences Using Sight Words

Let's practice reading sentences using our new sight words!

1. The dog is big.
2. An apple is red.
3. It is a sunny day.
4. I am at school.
5. The bird is in the cage.
6. A cat is on the table.
7. The boy and the girl are friends.
8. She is in the room.

Activity: Match the Sight Word to Its Sentence

Sight Word	Sentence
an	I see a dog.
the	An apple is red.
at	The sun is bright.
a	The dog is fast.
is	She is at school.
in	I like bread and butter.
on	The ball is in the box.
and	The cat is on the mat.

Activity: Read and Circle

Read each sentence carefully. Then, circle the sight words.

1. The dog is on the mat.
2. I see an apple.
3. It is a sunny day.

Activity: Sight Word Puzzles

Here are some simple puzzles to complete using our sight words:

Word Scramble

Unscramble the letters to form a sight word.

- **ta** → ________________
- **hes** → ________________
- **eh** → ________________
- **na** → ________________

Activity: Fill in the Missing Sight Word

Complete each sentence with the correct sight word from the list:

a, an, the, is, it, in, on, at, and

1. The dog ____________________ big.
2. I ___________________________ happy.
3. There is ____________________ book on the table.
4. She _______________________ running fast.
5. I am _______________________ the park.
6. The cat is __________________ the box.
7. The ball is _________________ the basket.
8. I like to play _______________ my friends.

Practice Makes Perfect

Activity: Create Your Own Sentences

Using the sight words listed, create your own sentences! Write at least two sentences with these words:

a, an, the, is, it, in, on, at, and

- Example:
  - **The dog is on the bed.**
  - **I am at school.**

Review: Look and Learn

Take a look at the words again! Can you read these sentences without stopping?

- **An apple is on the table.**
- **It is a sunny day.**
- **The cat is in the box.**
- **I am at the park with my friends.**

Quick Check:

Circle the correct word in the sentences:

1. I am ________________ home. (at, on)
2. The ball is ________ the table. (on, at)
3. I see ___________________ cat. (a, an)
4. She is _____________ the store. (in, at)

Chapter 4: High-Frequency Sight Words

Words We'll Learn in This Set:

The following high-frequency sight words are essential for building sentences and improving reading fluency. These words are **he**, **she**, **we**, **me**, **you**, **they**, **are**, **can**, **do**.

What Are High-Frequency Sight Words?

High-frequency sight words are words that appear very often in books, stories, and everyday reading. They are not always easy to sound out, so we recognize them by sight. These words are important because they help us understand sentences more quickly and smoothly.

Here's What These Words Do:

he: Refers to a boy or man.

- Example: **He is my brother**.

she: Refers to a girl or woman.

- Example: **She is my friend**.

we: Refers to a group of people including yourself.

- Example: **We are going to the park**.

me: Refers to yourself.

- Example: **Give it to me**.

you: Refers to the person you are talking to.

- Example: **You are my friend**.

they: Refers to a group of people or things.

- Example: **They are playing outside**.

are: A form of the word "be," used in sentences.

- Example: **You are happy.**

can: Means to be able to do something.

- Example: **I can jump high.**

do: Used to form questions or tell actions.

- Example: **Do you want to play?**

Did You Know?

The word "**are**" is one of the most important verbs in English! It helps describe what someone or something is doing or what something is like.

Activity: Fill in the Blank

Complete the sentences with the correct sight word from this list:

he, she, we, me, you, they, are, can, do

1. ________ like to read books. (we, you)
2. __________ is my best friend. (he, she)
3. _______ are playing soccer. (They, Me)
4. Can ____________ help me? (you, me)
5. ______________ can jump high. (I, she)
6. ______ are happy to see you. (We, You)
7. _________ do your homework. (I, We)
8. _____________ can sing well. (he, they)

Sentences Using Sight Words

Let's Practice Reading Sentences!

Here are some practice sentences using the words from Set 2:

He is my brother.

She is my friend.

We are going to the zoo.

You are my teacher.

They are running fast.

Can you jump high?

Do you like ice cream?

I can see the stars.

Activity: Match the Word to Its Sentence

Sight Word	Sentence
she	He is my friend.
we	She is in the classroom.
he	We are going to the store.
you	Can you help me?
they	You are my friend.
are	They are playing outside.
me	They are jumping.
do	I can do it.
can	What do you like?

Activity: Circle the Sight Words

Read the sentence below and circle the sight words you see:

"He can play with me and we are happy."

Activity: Word Scramble

Unscramble the letters to form the correct sight words.

1. **eh** → ____________________
2. **eshe** → ____________________
3. **ew** → ____________________
4. **em** → ____________________
5. **oayr** → ____________________
6. **ynat** → ____________________
7. **acn** → ____________________
8. **od** → ____________________

Activity: Sentence Building

Use the sight words to build sentences. You can arrange the words in any order to make a meaningful sentence.

Words: he, she, can, they, jump, we, run, do, play

- Example: **We can run.**

Now create your own sentences using these words:

1. ____

2. ____

3. ____

4. ____

Activity: Find the Missing Word

Read the sentence below. Fill in the missing word from this list:
he, she, we, me, you, they, are, can, do

1. I see ______________ cat.

2. They ____________ my friends.

3. __________ are playing outside.

4. Can you see ______________?

5. I ______________ like pizza.

Practice and Fun Activities

Activity: Read and Circle

Read these sentences and circle the sight words.

He is my brother.

She can run fast.

We are playing at the park.

They do their homework.

You are my friend.

Review Time: Look and Write

Can you remember the words we learned? Write them down:

1. ______________________________

2. ______________________________

3. ______________________________

4. ______________________________

5. ______________________________

Challenge!

Now that you've practiced these words, can you make your own sentences without looking at the examples? Write three sentences using these sight words:

1. ______________________________

2. ______________________________

3. ______________________________

Chapter 5:
Everyday Action Sight Words

Words We'll Learn in This Set:

In this set, we will focus on action words. These are words that tell us what someone or something is doing. They help us describe actions and are important for making sentences. The words we will cover are:

go, come, play, look, jump, run, eat, drink, sleep.

What Are Action Words?

Action words, also known as verbs, tell us about what someone or something is doing. These words help us describe actions in a story or in real life. Every time we want to explain what we or someone else is doing, we use action words.

For example:

Go means to move from one place to another.
- Example: **I go to school.**

Come means to move toward the speaker.
- Example: **Come here, please.**

Play means to engage in an activity for fun.
- Example: **I play with my friends.**

Look means to direct your eyes toward something.
- Example: **Look at the rainbow.**

Why Are Action Words Important?

Action words help us tell what is happening in the world around us. Without them, our sentences would be incomplete. Think about it: if we just said, "The dog," it doesn't really tell us what the dog is doing. But if we say, "**The dog runs**" or "**The dog sleeps**," now we know what the dog is doing!

Activity: Action Word Matching

Match the action word to the correct sentence. Draw a line between the word and the sentence.

Action Word	Sentence
play	I ________ to the park.
run	The children ________ in the yard.
go	The frog can ________ high.
eat	I ________ fast.
jump	I like to ________ apples.
sleep	She ________ water.
come	Can you ________ at the picture?
look	Please ________ inside.
drink	The cat is ready to ________ now.

Sentences Using Action Words

Practice Sentences with Action Words

Let's look at some sentences using the action words from this set. These sentences will help you understand how action words are used in everyday life.

1. **Go**
   - I go to school every day.
   - They go to the park after lunch.
2. **Come**
   - Please come inside, it's cold.
   - My friend will come over to play.
3. **Play**
   - I like to play with my dog.
   - They play soccer every Saturday.
4. **Look**
   - Look at that beautiful flower!
   - She looks at the stars at night.
5. **Jump**
   - I can jump over the puddle.
   - The kids jump on the trampoline.
6. **Run**
   - I run around the track every morning.
   - He runs fast like a cheetah.
7. **Eat**
   - I eat lunch at school.
   - We eat pizza for dinner.

8. **Drink**
   - She drinks water after running.
   - I drink milk with my cookies.

9. **Sleep**
   - The baby sleeps in a crib.
   - I sleep at night and wake up in the morning.

Activity: Create Sentences

Now that you've seen how these words are used, try creating your own sentences with these action words. Write at least one sentence for each action word.

Action Word: go
Sentence: ______________________________

Action Word: come
Sentence: ______________________________

Action Word: play
Sentence: ______________________________

Action Word: look
Sentence: ______________________________

Action Word: jump
Sentence: ______________________________

Action Word: run
Sentence: ______________________________

Action Word: eat
Sentence: ______________________________

Action Word: drink
Sentence: ______________________________

Action Word: sleep
Sentence: ______________________________

More Practice with Action Words

Activity: Fill in the Missing Word

Complete each sentence by filling in the blank with the correct action word from this list:

go, come, play, look, jump, run, eat, drink, sleep.

1. I want to ________________ to the store.
2. They ___________ together in the park.
3. He ______________ very fast in the race.
4. The dog likes to ________________ high.
5. I ___________ my breakfast at 7:00 AM.
6. Please _________________ at the picture.
7. After playing, I want to ___ some juice.
8. The baby is tired and ready to ________.
9. Can you ________________ here, please?

Activity: Read and Underline

Read the sentence and underline the action word.

1. The dog loves to play with a ball.
2. He can run very fast.
3. I eat breakfast in the morning.
4. She is drinking water.
5. I look at the sky.

Activity: Action Word Sorting

Write some action words and sort them into two categories:

"**Things I Do**" and "**Things Others Do**".

Things I do	Things Others Do

Activity: Action Word Sentences

Write a sentence using each of the following action words:

go, **come**, **play**, **look**, **jump**, **run**, **eat**, **drink**, **sleep**.

____

____

____

____

____

____

____

____

____

Activity: Action Word Picture Time

Draw a picture for any one of the sentences below.

- **I go to school every day.**
- **We play outside after lunch.**
- **The dog jumps over the fence.**
- **She eats her lunch at school.**

Chapter 6:
Descriptive Sight Words

Words We'll Learn in This Set:

In this set, we will focus on **descriptive words**—words that help us describe people, places, things, and actions. These words allow us to express how something is. The words we will cover are:

big, small, happy, sad, good, bad, fast, slow, up, down.

What Are Descriptive Words?

Descriptive words (also called adjectives) tell us more about a noun (person, place, or thing). They give us details about size, feelings, speed, direction, and quality. Without descriptive words, we wouldn't be able to fully understand the world around us.

For example:

Big describes something large in size.

- Example: **This is a big tree.**

Small describes something tiny or little.

- Example: **I have a small dog.**

Happy tells us about a good feeling.

- Example: **I feel happy today.**

Sad tells us about a feeling when something is wrong.

- Example: **She feels sad when it rains.**

Why Are Descriptive Words Important?

Descriptive words make our language more interesting. They help us to paint pictures with our words. Without these words, we wouldn't be able to say exactly what we mean. For example, instead of saying "The dog runs," we can say "The big dog runs fast," which tells us more about the dog and how it is running.

Activity: Descriptive Word Match

Match the descriptive word with its correct example.

Descriptive Word	Example Sentence
happy	The elephant is very ________________ .
good	The ant is ________________________ .
big	She feels ___________ when she smiles.
bad	The boy feels _________ after the game.
small	The food tastes ___________________ .
sad	This is a ______________________ idea.
up	The car is going __________________ .
down	The turtle moves _________________ .
slow	The balloon floated ________________ .
fast	The rain is falling _________________ .

Sentences Using Descriptive Words

Practice Sentences with Descriptive Words

Now, let's look at some sentences using the words from this set. These sentences help us see how to use descriptive words in everyday language.

Big

The giraffe is a **big** animal.
I saw a **big** truck on the road.

Small

The kitten is very **small**.
She has a **small** pencil case.

Happy

I feel **happy** when I play with my friends.
She looks **happy** in the picture.

Sad

He felt **sad** after the game.
The movie made me feel **sad**.

Good

This is a **good** idea!
I feel **good** after eating my vegetables.

Bad

This is a **bad** habit.
I had a **bad** day at school.

Fast

The cheetah runs very **fast**.
The train moves **fast**.

Slow

The snail moves **slow** across the garden.
The old car drives **slow**.

Up

The kite went **up** into the sky.
The bird flew **up** into the tree.

Down

The ball rolled **down** the hill.
I looked **down** at my shoes.

Activity: Fill in the Blanks

Complete each sentence using a word from the list:

big, small, happy, sad, good, bad, fast, slow, up, down.

1. The dog is very ____________________ .
2. She was _______ when she won the game.
3. The train is going ____________________ .
4. The boy ate a _________________ lunch.
5. The bird flew _____________ into the sky.
6. The car is moving ___________________ .
7. He has a ______________________ idea.
8. The ball bounced ____________ the stairs.
9. The mountain is very ________________ .
10. The mouse is too _______________ to see.

Activity: Sentence Building

Use the words below to create your own sentences. Write at least one sentence for each word.

Words: big, small, happy, sad, good, bad, fast, slow, up, down.

1. **Big:** ____
2. **Small:** ____
3. **Happy:** ____
4. **Sad:** ____
5. **Good:** ____
6. **Bad:** ____
7. **Fast:** ____
8. **Slow:** ____
9. **Up:** ____
10. **Down:** ____

More Practice with Descriptive Words

Activity: Match the Word to Its Meaning

Match each descriptive word to its meaning.

Descriptive Word	Meaning
sad	Something that is small.
good	Something that is large.
happy	A feeling when something is fun.
big	A feeling when something is wrong.
small	Something that is not good.
down	Something that is right.
bad	Moving quickly.
fast	Moving slowly.
slow	A direction going higher.
up	A direction going lower.

Activity: Descriptive Word Sorting

Sort the words into **positive** and **negative** categories.

Words: Happy, Bad, Sad, Good, Up, Fast, Slow, Down, Big, Small

Positive	Negative

Activity: Complete the Sentences

Complete these sentences with the right descriptive words from the list:

big, small, happy, sad, good, bad, fast, slow, up, down.

1. The car is moving very ________________ .
2. I feel ____________ when I eat my favorite food.
3. She is so ______________ after she got the gift.
4. The child is very ________ because he lost his toy.
5. The dog is very _____________ and likes to play.
6. The rain is falling ________________ .
7. The elephant is a very ______________ animal.
8. The snail is moving very ______________ .
9. The plane is flying ______________ in the sky.
10. The ball rolled ________________ the hill.

Review Time:

Now that you've learned many descriptive words, can you describe your favorite animal or place using these words? Write a few sentences:

1. ____
2. ____
3. ____

Chapter 7:
Sight Words for Colors and Numbers

What Are Colors and Numbers?

In this set, we will be learning about **colors** and **numbers**. Colors help us describe how things look, while numbers tell us how many things there are. Colors and numbers are important because they help us understand the world around us and help us describe what we see.

Colors We Will Learn:

The following colors will help you describe many things in your world:

red

blue

green

yellow

These are some of the first colors you see every day!

Numbers We Will Learn:

We will also be learning the first five numbers. Knowing these numbers will help you count and understand how many things there are.

one

two

three

four

five

Why Are Colors and Numbers Important?

Colors help us recognize objects, and numbers help us count them. Imagine you want to tell someone about your red ball or count how many yellow flowers are in the garden. Colors and numbers are essential parts of communication and learning!

Activity: Color and Number Match

Match the color or number to the correct description.

Color/Number	Description
one	A color of an apple.
green	The color of the sky.
yellow	The color of grass.
two	The color of the sun.
blue	The number of one apple.
red	The number of two hands.
five	The number of three dogs.
four	The number of four cars.
three	The number of five fingers.

Practice Sentences with Colors and Numbers

Sentences Using Colors

Here are some sentences that use colors. These will help you practice how to use color words in sentences.

Red

The apple is **red**.

I have a **red** balloon.

Blue

The sky is **blue**.

She wore a **blue** dress.

Green

The grass is **green**.

The frog is **green**.

Yellow

The sun is **yellow**.

I saw a **yellow** butterfly.

Sentences Using Numbers

Now let's practice using the numbers in sentences.

One

I have **one** book.

There is **one** bird in the tree.

Two

I see **two** cats.

She has **two** pencils.

Three

There are **three** apples on the table.

I have **three** friends at school.

Four

I see **four** chairs.

There are **four** cookies in the jar.

Five

There are **five** fingers on my hand.

I have **five** toys in my box.

Activity: Color and Number Sentences

Fill in the blanks with the correct color or number from the list:

red, blue, green, yellow, one, two, three, four, five.

1. The car is ______________________________ .
2. I have __________________ pencils in my bag.
3. The flower is ___________________________ .
4. There are ______________ books on the shelf.
5. The sky is _____________________________ .
6. The frog is ____________________________ .
7. I have _______________ apples in my basket.
8. The sun is _____________________________ .
9. I have ___________________________ shoes.
10. There are _______________ birds in the tree.

Fun Practice and Review

Activity: Draw and Label

Draw a picture using **two colors** and **three numbers**. Write a sentence about your drawing using the color and number words. For example, "I see **two red** apples and **three blue** birds."

1. Draw your picture here:

2. Write your sentence here: ______________________________

Review Time:

Now that you've learned color and number sight words, can you describe your favorite toy using these words? Write a few sentences below:

1. ______________________________
2. ______________________________
3. ______________________________

Chapter 8: Building Sentences with Sight Words

What Does Combining Sight Words Mean?

Combining sight words means putting two or more words together to form a complete sentence. This helps us make sense of what we are saying and writing. For example, let's combine some words from the previous sets to create new sentences!

Example Sentences Using Different Sets of Sight Words

Set 1: *a, an, the, is, it*

It is a sunny day.

The dog is big.

It is cold outside.

Set 2: *he, she, we, me, you*

He is my friend.

She is playing with the ball.

We are going to the park.

Set 3: *go, come, play, look, jump*

I **go** to school every day.

Look at the rainbow.

Let's **play** outside!

How to Build Sentences

To build sentences, follow these steps:

1. **Pick a subject** – The person or thing the sentence is about (e.g., I, she, dog).
2. **Choose a verb** – The action (e.g., run, play, is).
3. **Add more details** – Describe what the subject is doing or where (e.g., at the park, with a ball).

Combining More Sight Words

Combine Words from Sets 1, 2, and 3 to Make Sentences

Let's practice combining words from different sets.

1. **Set 1**: *a, an, the, is, it*
2. **Set 2**: *he, she, we, me, you*
3. **Set 3:** *go, come, play, look, jump*

Activity: Combine the Words to Make Sentences

Use the words from the boxes to create your own sentences. Write the sentences in the lines below.

Set 1	Set 2	Set 3
a	he	play
the	she	go
it	we	look
is	you	jump
an	me	come

For example, you can choose:

- **It** and **is** from Set 1
- **he** from Set 2
- **play** from Set 3

A sentence could be: "He **is playing**."

1. ______________________________

2. ______________________________

3. ______________________________

4. ______________________________

5. ______________________________

Sentence Completion Exercises

Fill in the Blanks with the Correct Sight Word

In this exercise, you will complete the sentences by choosing the correct sight word from the box. Think about what makes sense in the sentence.

Words: a, the, is, we, he, you, play, jump, look, at

1. I ____________________ go to the park.

2. The dog ____________________ run fast.

3. ____________ see the rainbow in the sky.

4. __________________ playing with a ball.

5. This is ______________________ apple.

6. We ________________ eat lunch together.

7. Do you ___________ the moon in the sky?

8. ______________ a big green frog jumping.

Build and Review Sentences

Create Your Own Sentences

Now, let's get creative! Use any of the sight words you've learned so far to make your own sentences.

1. Use **he** and **is** in a sentence.
   - Example: He **is** playing outside.

   Sentence: ____

2. Use **we** and **go** in a sentence.
   - Example: We **go** to the park.

   Sentence: ____

3. Use **it** and **look** in a sentence.
   - Example: **It** looks nice.

   Sentence: ____

4. Use **she** and **jump** in a sentence.
   - Example: **-** jumps high.

   Sentence: ____

Activity: Sentence Scramble

Unscramble the words to make a sentence.

1. is / ball / a / red / it ____
2. play / to / we / go / the / park ____
3. jumps / high / she ____
4. you / are / happy ____

Activity: Matching Sentences with Pictures

Look at the pictures below. Match the sentence to the correct picture by drawing a line from the sentence to the picture.

We go to the park.	
She looks at the stars.	
He jumps high.	
It is a red apple.	

Chapter 9:
Advanced Sight Words and Sentences

What Are Advanced Sight Words?

In this set, we will be learning **advanced sight words**. These words help us describe **relationships** between things, actions, or places. They are important because they allow us to create more **complex sentences**. Let's explore the following words:

- **because**
- **before**
- **after**
- **around**
- **under**
- **over**
- **near**
- **far**
- **together**
- **apart**

What Do These Words Mean?

Here are the meanings of each word and how we use them in sentences:

Because: Used to explain why something happens.

- Example: I went home **because** it was raining.

Before: Refers to something happening earlier in time.

- Example: I eat breakfast **before** I go to school.

After: Refers to something happening later in time.

- Example: We can play **after** our homework.

Around: Describes something moving or located on all sides.

- Example: The cat ran **around** the house.

Under: Describes something beneath or below.

- Example: The dog is hiding **under** the table.

Over: Describes something above or on top.

- Example: The airplane is flying **over** the city.

Near: Describes something that is close to something else.

- Example: The park is **near** my house.

Far: Describes something that is distant or far away.

- Example: The mountains are **far** from here.

Together: Describes two or more things being in one place or doing something as a group.

- Example: We are playing **together**.

Apart: Describes something being separated.

- Example: The pieces of the puzzle are **apart**.

Practice Sentences Using Advanced Sight Words

Practice with "Because"

- I wear a coat **because** it is cold outside.
- She cried **because** she lost her toy.
- We need to hurry **because** the bus is coming.

Practice with "Before"

- I brush my teeth **before** bed.

- We eat lunch **before** going outside.
- She finishes her homework **before** playing.

Practice with "After"

- We will go to the park **after** school.
- He took a nap **after** lunch.
- The movie starts **after** dinner.

Practice with "Around"

- The children ran **around** the playground.
- We walked **around** the park.
- The birds flew **around** the trees.

Practice with "Under"

- The ball rolled **under** the chair.
- The cat is hiding **under** the table.
- I found my shoe **under** the bed.

Practice with "Over"

- The helicopter flew **over** the building.
- He jumped **over** the puddle.
- The kite flew **over** the trees.

Building Sentences with Advanced Sight Words

Combine Advanced Sight Words to Create Sentences

Let's practice combining advanced sight words to form meaningful sentences.

Because + We + go

We go to the park **because** we like to play.

Before + She + eat

She eats lunch before going home.

After + I + read

I read a book after school.

Around + The children + play

The children play around the house.

Under + The dog + run

The dog runs under the table.

Over + The bird + fly

The bird flies over the park.

Activity: Complete the Sentences

Use the advanced sight words to complete these sentences:

1. The ball rolled ______________________________ the table.
2. I like to play with my friends _________________ school.
3. The dog ran _______________________________ the house.
4. We will eat dinner _________ we finish our homework.
5. She went to bed ___________________________ it was late.
6. We play ______________________ when we visit the park.
7. The book is __________________________________ the shelf.
8. The birds are flying __________________________ the trees.
9. I will do my homework ___________________ I watch TV.
10. We are sitting ___________________________ on the bench.

Advanced Sight Word Exercises

Activity 1: Word and Picture Matching

Match the sentence to the correct picture.

The books are on the table.	
We are playing together.	
She ran around the park.	
The dog is near the house.	
The airplane is flying over the mountains.	

Activity 2: Sentence Scramble

Unscramble the words to make a correct sentence. Write the sentences below.

1. ball / is / the / under / the / table

   ____

2. we / after / play / the / lunch

   ____

3. run / around / the / children / the / playground

   ____

4. the / bird / flew / over / the / house

   ____

5. she / because / cried / toy / her / lost

   ____

Activity 3: Write Your Own Sentences

Now, it's your turn! Choose at least **three advanced sight words** from the list and write your own sentences below:

Words: **because, before, after, around, under, over, near, far, together, apart**

1. ______________________________

   ____

2. ______________________________

   ____

3. ______________________________

   ____

Chapter 10:
Practice Activities

Activity 1: Read and Highlight

Read each sentence below aloud. Use a colored marker to highlight all the sight words in each sentence. Then, write down the sight words you found in a list.

1. The cat jumped over the wall.
2. We will play games after school.
3. The dog sat under the table.
4. I went to bed early because I was tired.
5. She ran around the park to catch her brother.
6. The boy was sitting near the door.
7. The plane is flying very far from here.
8. The teacher told us to stand apart during the game.

Activity 2: Identify and Write

Look at the highlighted sight words and write a sentence using each word.

Example: **Over** – The bird flew over the tree.

1. **Over** – ________________________________
2. **After** – ________________________________
3. **Under** – ________________________________
4. **Because** – ________________________________
5. **Around** – ________________________________
6. **Near** – ________________________________

Fill-in-the-Blank Practice

Activity 1: Fill the Blanks

Choose the correct sight word from the box to complete each sentence.

Sight Words: under, over, near, after, because, far, around

1. The cat hid ______________________________ the chair.
2. She smiled ___________________ her friend gave her a gift.
3. He jumped ______________ the puddle to avoid getting wet.
4. The stars in the sky are very _________________________.
5. The kids ran ______________ the playground during recess.
6. We will clean the room _______________________ lunch.
7. The dog sat _______________ the door waiting for its owner.

Activity 2: Create Sentences Around "Around"

Write sentences or examples of how the word "around" can be used in real life.

Example: "I walk **around** the garden every morning."

Sentence 1: _____________________________________

Sentence 2: _____________________________________

Sentence 3: _____________________________________

Sentence 4: _____________________________________

Sentence 5: _____________________________________

Writing and Matching Practice

Activity 1: Match the Sentences

Match the sight word to the sentence that uses it correctly.

Sight Word	Sentence
because	The book is ________________ the table.
under	The plane flew __________ the mountain.
near	I was late _________ the bus broke down.
over	The park is ________________ my house.

Activity 2: Write and Draw

Choose three sight words from the list below and write a sentence for each. Then draw a small picture to match each sentence.

Words to use: over, near, because

Sentence	Draw Here
1. Sentence: __________________________ __________________________	
2. Sentence: __________________________ __________________________	
3. Sentence: __________________________ __________________________	

Advanced Fill-in-the-Blanks

Activity 1: Fill in Longer Sentences

Complete the sentences by adding the correct sight word.

Sight Words: over, after, because, around, near

1. The kite is flying ______ the tree, and the children are chasing it.
2. We will go to the park ______ we finish our homework.
3. She was smiling ______ her friends surprised her with a cake.
4. The bench is ______ the fountain in the park.
5. The dog ran ______ the house to find its toy.

Activity 2: Write a Mini Paragraph

Write a short paragraph (3-4 sentences) using these sight words:

around, because, under

- Example:
  I walked **around** the park with my mom. We sat **under** the big tree to rest. I was happy **because** we had a fun time together.

Now write your paragraph:

____

____

____

____

____

Match Words to Pictures

Activity 1: Match the Word to the Correct Picture

Look at the pictures below and match them with the correct sight word from the word bank. Draw a line between the word and the picture.

Match the Word	Picture
Bag	
Pencil	
Parrot	
Elephant	
Book	

Fill-in-the-Blank Sentences with Pictures

Activity 1: Choose the Correct Word

Fill in the blanks with the correct sight word. Look at the pictures for clues.

1. The ______________________ is yellow.	
2. The ____________ is sitting under the tree.	
3. A ______________ is playing with the ball.	
4. There is a big ______________ in the park.	
5. The boy kicked the __________________.	

Activity 2: Sentence Writing

Write sentences about the pictures using sight words.

	Sentence: ______________________________
	Sentence: ______________________________
	Sentence: ______________________________
	Sentence: ______________________________
	Sentence: ______________________________

Fill in the Blanks with Sight Words

Activity 1: Complete the Sentences

Choose the correct sight word from the box to fill in the blanks.

Word Bank: a, the, is, on, at, run, look, play, in

1. The dog is ______________________ the bed.

2. I like to _____________________ in the park.

3. She will ______________ at the stars tonight.

4. This is _________________ beautiful flower.

5. The book is ____________________ the table.

6. He wants to ______ outside with his friends.

7. The cat is sleeping _____________ the basket.

8. Can we meet ___________ the mall at 5 PM?

Activity 2: Picture Clues

Fill in the blanks by looking at the pictures and using the correct sight words.

Word Bank: go, come, jump, eat

	He can ______________________ very high.
	She likes to ______________________ apples.
	The dog will ______________________ to the boy.
	Let's ______________________ for a ride.

Fill in the Blanks with Sight Words

Activity 1: Use the Words in Sentences

Pick a word from the box to complete each sentence.

Word Bank: happy, before, after, near, far, big, small, red, because

1. I am very __________ when I see my friends.
2. The tree is very ________________ and old.
3. The ball is ___________________ the chair.
4. We ate lunch ________________ the game.
5. I didn't go outside __________ it was raining.
6. The apple is _________________ and juicy.
7. My house is _____________ from the school.
8. This pencil is ______________ than that one.

Activity 2: Choose Your Own Words

Write your own sentences using the sight words below. Use each word once.

Words: because, happy, small, far

1. ____
2. ____
3. ____
4. ____

Word Search

Activity 1: Find the Words in the Puzzle

Search for the sight words in the grid below. Write sentences using the words you find.

Word List: a, the, is, in, on, at, look, play, jump

P	L	A	Y	I	N	K	J	U
A	T	H	E	I	S	O	N	J
J	I	A	T	L	O	O	K	M
U	M	P	J	U	M	P	N	P
B	C	A	I	N	P	L	S	Y

1. ____
2. ____
3. ____
4. ____
5. ____
6. ____
7. ____
8. ____
9. ____

Word Search

Activity 1: Find the Words in the Puzzle

Search for the sight words in the grid below. Words can be horizontal, vertical, or diagonal.

Word List: big, small, happy, red, blue, under, near, far, because

B	I	G	E	E	A	R	F	A
S	M	A	L	L	P	B	L	U
H	A	P	P	Y	R	E	D	E
U	N	D	E	R	F	A	R	C
N	E	A	R	B	E	C	A	U

Activity 2: Match the Word to the Sentence

Match the words found in the puzzle to their corresponding sentences.

Sentence	Word
The balloon is very ______________________.	near
I feel _____________ because it's my birthday.	big
The car is parked _______________ the house.	happy
She stayed home ____________ it was raining.	small
My hat is ______________ and not very large.	because

Unscramble the Words

Activity 1: Unscramble the Words

Rearrange the letters to form the correct sight word. Write the correct word in the blank.

1. **eht** → ____________________
2. **si** → ____________________
3. **ni** → ____________________
4. **yalp** → ____________________
5. **pjum** → ____________________

Activity 2: Use the Words in Sentences

Write a sentence using each unscrambled word.

Example:

- **The** cat is on the roof.
- I like to **play** soccer.

1. **the:** ____________________
2. **is:** ____________________
3. **in:** ____________________
4. **play:** ____________________
5. **jump:** ____________________

20 2-25

Unscramble the Words

Activity 1: Unscramble the Words

Rearrange the letters to form the correct sight word. Write the correct word in the blank.

1. **gbi** → ____________________
2. **ylhpa** → ____________________
3. **dre** → ____________________
4. **unrde** → ____________________
5. **ftra** → ____________________

Activity 2: Match the Word to the Sentence

Match the unscrambled words to their corresponding sentences.

Sentence	Word
The apple is ____________________.	big
The elephant is very ________________.	red
The box is ________________ the table.	happy
I am very ____________________ today!	far
The school is __________ from my house.	under